THE NILE FILES

Stories about Ancient Egypt

THE FEARFUL PHARAOH

by Philip Wooderson

Illustrations by Andy Hammond

W

FR... ...TS
NE... ...NEY

First published in 2000 by Franklin Watts
96 Leonard Street, London EC2A 4XD

Text © Philip Wooderson 2000
Illustrations © Andy Hammond 2000

The right of Philip Wooderson to be identified as
the Author of this Work has been asserted by
him in accordance with the Copyright, Designs
and Patents Act, 1988

Editor: Lesley Bilton
Designer: Jason Anscomb
Consultant: Dr Anne Millard, BA Hons, Dip Ed, PhD

A CIP catalogue record for this book
is available from the British Library

ISBN 0 7496 3651 3 (hbk)
0 7496 3655 6 (pbk)

Dewey Classification 932

Printed in Great Britain

CONTENTS

A QUICK WORD IN YOUR EAR

After thirty years on the throne, Pharaoh Armenlegup (known as The Fearful Pharaoh) is about to celebrate the Festival of Sed.

THIS WON'T BE MUCH FUN FOR HIM.

He will have to sprint around a race course, watched by important guests who have come from far and wide. Only if he can make it to the finishing line will there be rejoicing and Good Omens for thirty more years on the throne. Then Pharaoh can put his feet up and enjoy the rest of the party.

P.S. THIS IS THE TRUTH.

"Made it," grinned Dad. "Perfect timing!"

Dad's crew weren't looking so happy. In front of them stretched a long line of larger boats, waiting to unload their goods at the quay.

"We're going to be last," said one of the lads.

"As usual."

"No we aren't," said Dad, giving the

steering oar a sudden twist. *Hefijuti* cut smartly in front of a grand sleek galley, packed with soldiers wielding spears.

"Hey. Where do you think you're going?" bellowed their captain, glaring down at Dad.

"Same place as you," Dad called back. "And we've got a load of fine wines to deliver to Pharaoh – so it's urgent!"

The quay was already crowded with folk in colourful costumes and piles of sacks and boxes. There were even some big wooden cages containing exotic beasts. Ptoni counted five monkeys, a panther and one baby giraffe.

"Pharaoh buys lots of pets," said Dad, glancing at Ptiddles, the ship's cat. "Perhaps we could gain favour by throwing in –"

"No we couldn't," said Ptoni, as Ptiddles shot up the mast.

Three guards were checking through all the cargo as it was unloaded, and a scribe was scribbling notes.

"That's Anubit's last item of luggage. Now let's move on to her gifts. Three cases of prime ostrich plumes –"

"So who's this new bit then?" Dad asked the scribe.

"*Princess Anubit* is from Nubia.* She's only just disembarked. Met by the Pharaoh in person, along with his eldest son. So show some respect," said the scribe, turning back to business. "Gifts of the rarest perfumes, gold goblets encrusted with jewels, unusual Nubian wildlife –"

* Nubia was next to Egypt – see page 60

" No wine," whispered Dad to Ptoni. "Looks like we might be in luck."

"Hold on, Dad. He said *gifts*."

"*Gifts*?" Dad repeated. "Quite right. It's always best on occasions like these to give Pharaoh some small trinket." He tapped the side of his nose. "Oils the wheels of commerce. In fact, this could be our chance to get rid of that mummified cat we picked up at the shrine. We'll wrap it up so that it looks smart."

"It's already wrapped. It's a mummy. And, anyway," Ptoni stopped and looked round him, "it won't look very impressive compared with encrusted goblets and –"

"Okay, okay." Dad was unphased. "We'll just pop it in a big box and leave it on the quay."

"And hope the guards don't look inside."

"I'll make sure of that," said Dad. "You see that basket over there, between the giraffe and the monkey?"

"The one with the drawing of the snake on its side?"

"Yes. What sort of fool would lift the lid and take a look in that?"

"Right, Dad, but a mummified cat's not as dangerous as a snake."

"Ptoni," said Dad, "do you really think that there's a snake in that basket? More likely something precious, like a headdress encrusted with jewels, that the princess doesn't want stolen. So we'll draw a snake on our box too. In fact we'll go one better. We'll pop your pet snake inside."

Ptoni wavered. "Are you sure, Dad?"

"Positive. All the top traders take these safety precautions."

As Ptoni reluctantly brought out Rasp, his pet snake, he heard a great fit of squealing

from one of the palace windows.

"Ooh, look at that little chap."

"He's got an enormous snake."

"What's his weedy chum up to?"

Dad raised his hand. "Dear ladies, please don't be alarmed. This snake is a pet – it's quite harmless."

He turned back to
Ptoni and winked. "You know who
they are? Some of Pharaoh's wives. Queen
Mudpat's the one in the hat. I think I made
quite an impression on them. But then, you see,
I'm an expert on how to make friends at the
palace."

"So what are we going to do next, Dad?"

"We'll leave our gift here, while we go and

find the Head Wine Man and give him some wine to sample. Right, Ptoni, you carry the jar."

It wasn't easy to find the way – there were so many doorways and alleys. But finally they ended up in an enormous courtyard.

"The Festival site," said Dad.

On the left was a platform, shaded by canopies, with lots of colourful pennants flapping in the hot breeze. On the right were a number of booths painted with hieroglyphs. Ptoni guessed these were shrines to the gods.

"Refreshment stalls!" Dad rubbed his hands. "That's where they'll be serving our wines."

He opened the nearest doorway, but found his way blocked by a man who looked down at Ptoni's jar. "Is that the sacred oil for the shrine?" he asked politely.

"No," Dad breathed in sharply. "It's sacred *wine*. The best vintage. I can let you have thirty flasks."

The young man shook his head sadly.

"At a keen discount," Dad added. "Specially for you."

The man was wearing the finest robes and the most costly jewellery. But he was thin and pale, with eyes like muddy puddles.

"My name is Pitterpat."

"That's not your fault," said Dad, patting his back. "I once had a friend called Vomit, but that never held him back. He runs a small brewery now." Dad laughed. "You should count your blessings."

With a sorry sigh, Pitterpat told them that he'd been appointed Priest In Charge of the Festival.* "As such it is my job to make sure the Pharaoh gets round the course."

"And I'm sure you will," said Dad.

"Then I'm responsible for the celebrations."

* The Festival of Sed was very important – see page 61

"We saw all the gifts," said Dad, "and left our own magnificent offering on the quay. It'll be like a birthday party."

"Except it's a wedding," sighed Pitterpat.

"Who's getting married?" asked Dad.

"Pharaoh, of course."

"But he's married," said Ptoni, glancing at Dad. "I mean he's *very* married. How many wives has he got?"

"Twenty-nine," moaned Pitterpat. "But this

is his thirtieth year on the throne, so he wants a thirtieth bride. Urgh!"

Dad looked sympathetic. "Eaten something that disagreed with you?"

"Yes. The food of love!" Pitterpat groaned. "She's just arrived at the palace – the most beautiful girl in the world – and it was love at first sight."

"Oh dear." Dad shook his head sagely. "You're a nice enough lad, but you've got no chance against Pharaoh – besides, she's a Nubian princess!"

"But I can't live without her!"

"There are plenty more pretty young girls." Dad gave him a dig in the ribs. "Why I saw one only this morning, selling watermelons, and she –"

SQUEEZE ME!

"OY, YOU!" a voice yelled from the courtyard. "Who do you think you're nudging?"

Ptoni turned to see three angry guards.

"He says he's called Pitterpat, poor chap," said Dad grinning at the guards. "My goodness, he's got problems."

The Head Guard drew his sword. "He's not the only one. That's *Prince* Pitterpat you're talking about. The King's-Eldest-Son-Of-His-Body-Whom-He-Dearly-Loves. And, what's more, Queen Mudpat is his mother."

Dad spun round. "The King's . . . Queen Mudpat's . . . Help!" Falling on his knees, he dragged Ptoni down beside him. "Wasn't I only just saying that this handsome young man has such a royal aura? And I wasn't nudging him. I'd spotted a small piece of dirt –"

"Who are you calling a piece of dirt?"

"Please," Prince Pitterpat turned to the guards. "This poor fellow's only been trying to cheer me up – in his own simple way. And he says he's got some fine wines to trade. Take him to meet the Head Storeman."

"It's our lucky day," Dad whispered as the guards led them through a maze of narrow alleyways. They emerged in a yard where servants were kneading bread dough, watched over by a plump little man holding a rolled-up scroll.

"What do you want?" he demanded.

"We bring some rare wines," Dad told him. "We thought, if you're the Head Storeman, you should have the honour of being the first to enjoy them."

Ptoni pulled the bung from his flask and poured some wine into a goblet provided by one of the servants.

The storeman swirled it about, took a small sip, tried to gargle, then spat it out with a cough.

Dad gave an approving nod. "The best tasters all do that, Ptoni. It keeps their palettes clear."

"Indescribable!" gasped the storeman, clutching at his throat.

"Ambrosia?" suggested Dad. "Sun-kissed peaches, perhaps, with a subtle hint of almonds?"

The storeman spat again. "I wouldn't use this in the kitchen. Not even for scouring the pots."

"Neither would I," agreed Dad. "No, this should be kept back for Pharaoh himself."

"Don't you dare to mention His Highness,"

roared the Head Guard. "You scum!"

"B-but, he's Pitterpat's Dad, and any friend of Pitterpat's –"

"Don't push it!" The Head Guard was bristling. "You're already in big trouble for mooring your crummy boat and leaving a dangerous snake on the palace quay."

"It's not dangerous, and anyway it was guarding our gift for Pharaoh, a valuable sacred cat – sure to bring good luck."

The guard gave Dad a withering glare. "And you're going to need it, sunshine."

CHAPTER 3
PHARAOH'S WIVES

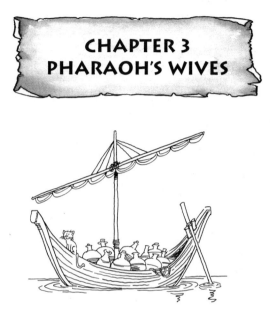

The guards dragged Dad across the quay.

All the barges had been unloaded and their crews were lounging on deck drinking beer. All except *Hefijuti* – its deck was still crowded with wine pots. Where were the lads, Ptoni wondered.

"Open this," said the Head Guard, whacking the box with his sword.

"It's been opened already," gasped Dad,

lifting the lid. Ptoni peered inside. Shifting a handful of straw he uncovered the cat's bandaged head.

"Ah good! Pharaoh's gift is still there," exclaimed Dad, lifting out the cat and cradling it like a baby.

"We don't want that mangy object!" The Head Guard grabbed the cat by the neck and chucked it into the river. "Hurry up! Where's the snake?"

Rasp was not in the box.
"Does Pharaoh like snakes?" Dad asked.
The Head Guard raised his sword and

looked closely at Dad. "Don't you understand, numb-skull? Snakes are strictly forbidden anywhere near the palace."

"There's another one just over there." Dad pointed across the quay.

"It's gone," Ptoni whispered. "Along with the monkeys, the panther and the baby giraffe."

"That's enough. I want this boat searched!" yelled the guard. His men rushed about, peering deep into the wine pots, and poking their spears under sacks.

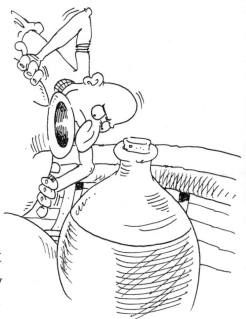

"Funny things snakes," Dad murmured, fishing over the side of the boat for the mummified cat. "I mean, when you don't want to see them, they always get under your feet."

"Let's hope you find it as funny being locked up for the night." The guard turned back to Ptoni. "As for you," he scowled, "you've got until dawn tomorrow to find that snake – dead or alive. Or else your useless father is going to be buried up to his scrawny neck in sand, and left for the vultures' breakfast."

When Dad had been dragged away, protesting loudly, Ptoni sat on the deck stroking Ptiddles, who'd just scrambled down the mast.

Where could Rasp have got to?

He looked round to
see the lads clambering
unsteadily onto the boat.

"We've just done a deal –"

"With Pharaoh's wives –"

"Great bunch of women –"

"One of them wanted an unusual pet, so –"

"You didn't sell Rasp?" shouted Ptoni.

"Your Dad owes us six months' wages –"

"Oh, shut up!" Dodging round them, Ptoni
jumped ashore. He hurried across the quay and
darted through a doorway, up some stairs into
the palace. Tiptoeing past a guard who was

cleaning his toenails with his dagger, Ptoni went through room after room. He was following the sound of women's voices.

At last, peering round an archway, he caught sight of Pharaoh's wives.

They were all squabbling and giggling until Queen Mudpat shouted. "We've now got a wonderful chance to take revenge on Pharaoh, thanks to those idiots who sold me this snake."

"B-but we might get blamed, Queen Mudpat."

"I'll make sure Anubit gets blamed. She actually brought a poisonous snake as one of her gifts to Pharaoh! Don't worry, the goddess will be on our side."

"Which one?"

"The goddess Hathor."

"But Hathor's the goddess of Love –"

"And of Beauty, Queen Mudpat."

"Exactly. She will help us get revenge on Pharaoh for scorning *our* love – and *my* beauty."

Silence.

Ptoni couldn't be sure what Queen Mudpat was plotting, but it was obvious she didn't want to be overheard. It wouldn't be wise to be caught here and taken for a spy. But as he tried to back out, his foot caught a table leg, knocking a pottery oil lamp on to the floor.

"Who's there?"

He shrank behind the wall hanging, hoping he didn't bulge out. But then he felt something furry brushing his shin. He tried to kick Ptiddles away, but he missed. Then he heard footsteps coming up the stairs.

The guard pulled back the hanging. "OY, what have we here?"

Queen Mudpat loomed up behind the guard. She was as round as a boulder, with an angry red leathery face under her frightening headdress.

"Your Highness," blurted Ptoni, falling to his knees. "I'm sorry if I scared you. I only came to ask you if some men sold you my snake. You see, Rasp's my pet and –"

The other wives started to giggle.

"Rubbish!" snapped the Queen. "The boy's just a lying thief. Take him away. Chop his head off."

The guard dragged Ptoni downstairs. But when they got to the bottom he suddenly loosened his grip. "Right. Now listen to me. I'm going to take you to the chief. We've had a shrewd suspicion those wives were up to new tricks – and if you overheard something it might just save your head, and spare your Dad being buried in sand . . . and earn me a bit of promotion. So everyone's happy. Let's go."

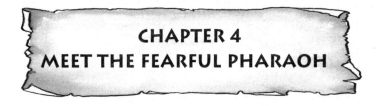

CHAPTER 4
MEET THE FEARFUL PHARAOH

The guard dragged Ptoni down a dark echoing passage, into a gloomy hall with oil lamps flickering in niches. At the far end of the chamber was a low platform with a gigantic canopied throne. Ptoni could hear puffs and grunts coming from somewhere behind it. Strange shadows loomed over the flagstones. His heart was thumping as he thought of the Fearful Pharaoh.*

* Pharaoh had the top job – see page 62

The guard pushed him forward. Screwing up his courage, Ptoni took the last few steps round the back of the throne, into the Pharaoh's presence. He stopped short in amazement. In front of him were two slaves flapping feathery fans over a thin, wizened little man who was trying to do sit-ups. A big, flabby fellow with a pasty face was holding

TWENTY SIX, TWENTY SEVEN, TWENTY EIGHT,

down his feet and counting out loud. "Come on sire, remember you've got to run round the course at the Festival tomorrow."

"I'm hardly likely to forget it!" gasped the little man, fighting for his breath.

"Who's that?" Ptoni whispered.

"That's the Fearful Pharaoh, you fool, and his Chief Minister, Donut. Bow down,"

growled the guard. "Quick! Grovel!"

The Pharaoh sat up with a groan and a slave wiped his brow. "What have we here?"

The guard muttered something to Donut, who murmured in Pharaoh's ear. Pharaoh's left eye started twitching.

"You say you've found a spy in my wives' private quarters? How clever. How did you do that?"

"Please, Your Highness, I just went to ask your wives if they happened to have my pet sna –"

Donut's hand clamped round his mouth.

"Snail," said Donut firmly.

"You've got a pet *snail*?" asked Pharaoh. "How charming. What's he called?"

Donut removed his hand.

"Rasp, but he's not a snail. He's a –"

"SSSSSHHHH!"

Donut hissed so loudly he nearly exploded.

Pharaoh went white and his hands flew up to his cheeks. "The boy's not lost a sss . . .?"

"Snake," said Ptoni. "Yes I have. But don't worry, he's quite harmless."

"Oh–urgh! I feel faint and dizzy."

Donut glared at Ptoni.

"It's only the truth," Ptoni blurted.

"The truth?" Donut cried, pulling Ptoni into a dark corner. "The truth," he carried on in a threatening whisper, "is that Pharaoh's so fearful of you-know-whats, that the very word turns him to jelly."

It suddenly all made sense. Ptoni understood why the guards had been so worried about the snake, and why they had dragged Dad off. "We didn't know. Dad meant no harm, sire."

Pharaoh took no notice. "As if this wretched festival wasn't bad enough, without my wives having a sssecret . . ."

"Pharaoh's wives are jealous," said Donut turning back to Ptoni, "because Princess

Anubit is such a gorgeous young woman. So we need to know what they're plotting."

"It's clear as day," screamed Pharaoh. "They'll let it squirm in here and –"

"Hold on, sire." Ptoni broke in, aware that this might be his only chance to save his Dad from the vultures.

"They won't let it go. They'll *keep* it."

"Whatever for?" scoffed Donut.

"To put on the course, of course. They'll hide it there tomorrow – to stop Pharaoh getting round."

There was a shocked silence.

"The lad is right," groaned Donut. "They're such

cunning devils. They'll hide it in one of the shrines that Pharaoh has to run into on his way round the course."

Pharaoh was biting his knuckles. "Oh, why did I ever agree to take on a thirtieth wife?"

"She brings great wealth," said Donut.

"And a baby giraffe," ventured Ptoni.

"It's too late to call off the wedding without great loss of face. The only thing to do is to catch the sss . . ."

"Silly thing," finished Ptoni.

Donut looked at him slightly more kindly.

"It'll soon be dark," Pharaoh snivelled.

"We could set some traps," said the guard.

"Brilliant," said Donut. "*You* can set the traps, and if you manage to catch it, I'll see you get promoted."

CHAPTER 5
SSS-SORTED?

That night Ptoni had to stay up and keep watch in Pharaoh's chamber, because Pharaoh still half-expected a snake to slip into his bed. The floor was as hard as stone and Pharaoh had noisy dreams.

"Help, there's a sss . . ."

"Mercy! Mudpat!"

Ptoni had his own wide-awake nightmares, wondering what would happen if Rasp wasn't caught in a trap. But he must have dozed off in the end, because when he opened his eyes next, Pharaoh was doing more sit-ups and the chamber was full of sunshine.

Then the guard entered the room, bearing a basket. "I've got it, sire. I've caught your s –"

"Ssssplendid," Donut cried, letting go of the royal ankles.

Pharaoh tipped back with a thud.

"You mean I'm s-s-safe?"

"That's right, Your Highness. You can get round the course without any fear on that subject. And I can have my promotion."

Pharaoh stood up, looking dazed.

"No sss . . . sticking its fangs into me?"

"No danger at all," declared Donut.

Pharaoh whistled and danced a quick jig. "Tee hee!" Grabbing hold of Ptoni, he kissed him on both cheeks. "You clever boy, what can I do for *you*?"

Ptoni took a quick breath. "Could you please not bury my Dad in the sand."

"Consider it done. Set his Dad free."

As the guard hurried off to do this, there was a noisy fanfare of horns and a great procession of scribes streamed in, followed by Pitterpat.

Pharaoh greeted him brightly. "Cheer up, Eldest-Son-Of-My-Body. The sss has been sorted. Let's go!"

"We wish luck to your Highness," said Donut.

Pitterpat only managed a sigh as the procession moved off, with Pharaoh striding ahead, leaving Donut and Ptoni (and the basket containing the snake).

From the window they had a good view of the tents and the shrines in the courtyard, with the raised platform opposite, so they could watch the important guests waiting to take their seats.

Donut pointed out Princess Anubit with her retinue in bright robes gathering at one end, and twenty-nine grim-faced wives down the other end, bunched up round Queen Mudpat. But, as the horns started blaring again, Ptoni stepped back from the window to take a quick peep in the basket. He wanted to make sure Rasp was all right.

PSSSSSSSSSSS!!!!!! The snake reared up.

But it wasn't harmless Rasp. This was a poisonous snake.* A deadly horned viper! One bite and you'd be lucky to live for another three minutes – never mind thirty years! Ptoni slammed the lid down. Where on earth was Rasp?

Cheering broke out from the courtyard.

"Come on, quick. It's starting," called Donut. Ptoni rushed back to the window.

Pharaoh leapt the first two hurdles and bounded towards the first booth like a young antelope.

"Shrine of Isis," Donut shouted into a cone-shaped tube that amplified his voice over the heads of the crowd. "God of Death and Rebirth." Then he turned and whispered to Ptoni. "That's the place where the guard trapped your snake. Lucky for your Dad, though not for the buzzards. Tee hee!"

* Egyptian snakes could be highly dangerous – see page 63

Ptoni didn't think it was funny. Rasp was still out there somewhere. His eye was caught by Mudpat, straining forward as Pharaoh came sprinting out. Her gaze didn't flinch. She was waiting – waiting for something to happen.

Then Ptoni saw Princess Anubit tugging her chunky earrings and looking across at Pitterpat. He remembered Mudpat saying that a dangerous snake had been one of her gifts. Perhaps Anubit had hidden it in the sacred booth, hoping it would bite Pharaoh because she couldn't bear the thought of marrying such an old man? But it had been caught in the trap that had been meant for Rasp.

"Great Pharaoh takes the last lap easily in his stride," Donut declared to the crowd as

Pharaoh lurched over a hurdle, knocking it hard with his shin.

He didn't look quite so perky now, with sweat dribbling down his cheeks and veins pulsing all over his forehead. He was fighting for breath. He was gasping. He nearly tripped up, but he staggered on – into the final booth.

"The shrine of Hathor," boomed Donut. "Goddess of Love and Beauty!"

Ptoni winced. Mudpat sucked her cheeks in. The other wives all leant forward.

Then there was a terrible scream.

"YAAAAAAAAAAAA!"

"And he's out!" cried Donut.

CHAPTER 6
SSS-SPECIAL EFFECTS

Mudpat jumped to her feet, knocking off her headdress, but that didn't stop her from grinning. As for all the junior wives, they were flapping about like small birds, twittering with excitement. Even Pitterpat managed a smile, though it was soon wiped from his face as Pharaoh bolted at top speed across the finishing line. The crowd erupted with wild cheers.

"Yes, Pharaoh has made it," boomed Donut. "And what an amazing last spurt. Good Omens for thirty more years of Pharaoh's Glorious Reign."

Pharaoh collapsed in the dust. He lay there panting for breath, gasping out "Ssssssend that boy to me!"

Donut's hand fell on Ptoni's shoulder. "He's thinking of you. What an honour."

As he was led through the crowd, Ptoni only expected the honour of being buried in sand next to Dad. Though Dad didn't look too

worried. Ptoni could see him helping to lift Pharaoh onto a couch. Slaves gathered round with towels, ready to rub him down, while others started to fan him with plumes of ostrich feathers.

Then Donut was booming again. "Now the gods have shown their pleasure in Pharaoh's great fitness and health, I am proud to announce Pharaoh's plans for a Royal Wedding!"

Mudpat and the wives did not look very pleased.

Prince Pitterpat looked even less pleased. Princess Anubit looked *desperate*.

And then Ptoni saw two guards lugging another basket out of the shrine of Hathor.

Pharaoh pointed a shaky finger. "Do you know what's inside that basket? It nearly scared me to death."

"But my pet helped you to finish," cried Ptoni.

"Your pet?" Pharaoh croaked. "But if that's yours, where did the other one come from?"

"It was her gift," bellowed Mudpat waving a fist at Anubit. "I'd chop off her head!"

Pharaoh darted a glance at the unhappy princess, before looking back at Queen Mudpat and his other twenty-eight wives.

"You monsters don't want me to marry again, but neither does my bride to be. Or not to be. That is the question." He wiped his brow. He was trembling. "But if I back out now, everyone will titter. Oh, what am I going to do?"

Ptoni screwed up his face, trying his best to look puzzled, but there was an easy answer. "Please sire, excuse me saying, but why don't you ask Pitterpat . . ."

"Ask him what?"

Ptoni took a deep breath. "If he'd marry her for you."

Pharaoh blinked. "For me, you mean? Just to help his old Dad?"

"He'll do as he's told," said Donut. "I mean, Pitterpat's very loyal."

"Loyal to ME," Mudpat cried out. "He's my eldest son as well and he'll do whatever I tell him!"

"How helpful," murmured Pharaoh, wiping more sweat from his brow.

Donut cleared his throat. "So as I was saying, I'm proud to announce Pharaoh's plan for the beautiful Princess Anubit to wed Prince Pitterpat, the King's-Eldest-Son-Of-His-Body-Whom-He-Loves-More-Dearly-Than-Ever!"

Mudpat sat down with a grunt. Pitterpat gawped at the princess, a huge smile spread across her face. And then he was running towards her. And soon they were hugging and

kissing. And everyone else was cheering,
"Great Pharaoh is fearful, but wise, too!" and
Pharaoh was blushing. "It'sssss nothing."

The wedding took place on the next day.

Ptoni and Dad were asked to the banquet. They sat at the lowliest table, but in the middle of the feast Donut came down to join them.

"A message from Pharaoh," he murmured. "As a small token of his thanks for things turning out so well, he commands you to collect and transport to him the taxes due from two of his Royal farms."

Dad frowned "Is he going to pay us to do that?"

Donut winced. "The dues should be worth a small fortune, dimwit, and you'll get ten percent of them."

Dad threw a quick glance at Ptoni. "Ah well," he suddenly grinned, "in that case the answer is yes. I knew we'd do well at the palace. Didn't I tell you, Ptoni?"

"Yes, Dad."

"When you know the ropes as well as I do, Ptoni, there's nothing to be afraid of. Not even a Fearful Pharaoh!"

Nubia

The country of Nubia lay to the south of
Egypt, and it was ruled by Egypt for many
centuries. Nubians were great traders selling
ostriches, apes, leopard skins, giraffes' tails,
ebony and ivory.

The Festival of Sed

The Festival of Sed happened after a Pharaoh had reigned for thirty years. It showed that he was still fit to wear the crown and confirmed his right to rule. Spectators from all over the country gathered at the palace and cheered as the Pharaoh ran round a special course. When he succeeded (as he always did) then he was recrowned. The celebrations lasted for weeks and the whole country came to a standstill.

Pharaohs

The Egyptians called their kings "Pharaohs".
The word means "the Great House" in
Egyptian and referred to the palace. The
position of Pharaoh was inherited, and passed
to the eldest son of the Pharaoh's chief wife.

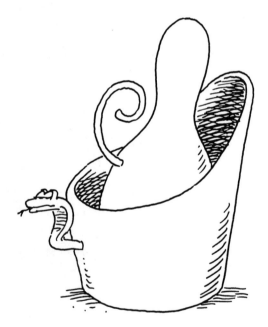

Snakes

Work in the fields meant Egyptians might be bitten by several kinds of snake. The sand and horned vipers were particularly dreaded. Death followed a few minutes after their bite. The cobra was regarded as a particularly powerful snake, and a replica of one adorned all the Pharaoh's crowns.

Join Ptoni and his Dad up the Nile
in these other books.

THE SCRUNCHY SCARAB

07496 3649 1 (Hbk)   07496 3653 X (Pbk)

The town of Feruka is having a big celebration, but all Dad
has to sell are some dried-up figs and a few old flasks of oil.
Fortunately Ptoni finds a lucky scarab beetle – so perhaps
things will change for the better?

THE MISSING MUMMY

07496 3650 5 (Hbk)   07496 3654 8 (Pbk)

Dad goes to collect some wine he is owed by Slosh, the
merchant. But poor Slosh has died, and someone has stolen
his mummy. It's up to Ptoni to find it, and to claim the wine.

THE HELPFUL HIEROGLYPH

07496 3652 1 (Hbk)   07496 3656 4 (Pbk)

Dad decides that it's time Ptoni learnt to read and write, so
he hires an old scribe to teach him. Ptoni's new knowledge
of hieroglyphs helps him sort out a very peculiar mystery.